Inspirational Stories
for the Young Reader

Inspirational Stories for the Young Reader

BETTINA DIGIULIO

RESOURCE *Publications* • Eugene, Oregon

INSPIRATIONAL STORIES FOR THE YOUNG READER

Resource Publications
An Imprint of Wipf and Stock Publishers
199 W. 8th Ave., Suite 3
Eugene, OR 97401

www.wipfandstock.com

PAPERBACK ISBN: 978-1-7252-7740-3
HARDCOVER ISBN: 978-1-7252-7739-7
EBOOK ISBN: 978-1-7252-7741-0

Manufactured in the U.S.A.   07/27/20

This book is dedicated to my daughter, Stephanie,
her husband, Tyler, and my granddaughter Isabella,
and to all my former students
who made my teaching years enjoyable.

Contents

Acknowledgments

THANK YOU TO GEORGE Duma who encouraged me to have these stories published.

Thank you to Sandy Johnson for her computer knowledge and assistance in preparing this manuscript for publication.

Thank you to Megan Gravely for the illustrations in this book.

The Treasure

Forgiveness is the final form of love.

—Reinhold Niebuhr

Francesco glanced at the clock above the chalkboard. *Five more minutes until freedom*, he thought. Making eye contact with Brian across the aisle, he whispered, "I'll meet you at the quarry in fifteen minutes."

Brian nodded approval. As he put his books away, he heard Tamika whispering to Francesco, "You boys should *not* be fishing at the quarry."

Brian glared at her and whispered, "It's none of your beeswax what we do, so just butt out."

With a jerk of her head, Tamika turned away.

As the dismissal bell rang, Miss Bailey announced, "Don't forget, your rock projects are due tomorrow."

"Yes Miss Bailey," they all chorused.

The boys were physical opposites. Blonde haired and green eyed, Brian was short and stocky and looked as if he'd be a good wrestler. Almost a head taller and lanky, Francesco's Italian heritage showed in his black hair and big brown eyes, fringed by long lashes. By their teens both would turn girls' heads. Best friends since kindergarten, they did everything together, liked the same things, hated the same things, and had no secrets between them—that they knew of.

At the bicycle rack they grabbed their bikes and peddled home to change clothes and get their fishing gear. Arriving at the abandoned quarry, they settled down at the edge of the bank, baited their hooks, cast their lines, and waited patiently for a bite.

The long-abandoned quarry was their escape into nature. A small forest surrounded the flooded pit with rocky banks. Plants and ferns grew among the tailings and at the forest's edge; seagulls and geese searched for food. The boys would see fish leap from the quarry water and watch the gulls swoop down and snatch them. Sometimes the boys brought along bread for these scavengers. The graceful flight of the gulls captivated them, and they fantasized flying with them high above the clouds.

They spent hours searching the perimeters for unusual rocks to add to their collection.

"Look at all the shale and sandstone around here," Francesco pointed.

"I'll bet no one can top what we have in our project," Brian said, grinning.

"Nosy Tamika was butting into our business again," said Francesco. "I hope she and Big Mouth Jillian don't come around here bothering us."

"Oh, they'll be around, especially if they know we are here," said Brian. "Let's go farther down. We might get lucky and catch something. There's nothing here."

Rambling along the bank, kicking at loose rocks, Francesco saw something unusual. "Look at that rock," he said as he reached for it. "It looks like the trilobite in Miss

Bailey's fossil book. It is—it's a real trilobite." It just fit in the palm of his hand.

They could clearly see the head, the thin bony spine, and tail sections imprinted on the thin grey shale. Running their fingers along the rock, the boys observed its segmented body, which proved it was a trilobite.

"Wow, it's the real thing," Brian whispered, awed by their find.

They immediately began to speculate on their future with this treasure.

"We could donate it to the museum, and we'll be on the news! We'll be famous," said Francesco.

Just then, they heard the girls coming.

"Quick, hide it," whispered Francesco. "If they see it, they'll blab to everyone." Francesco tucked the stone into some tall weeds on the bank.

"Get lost," ordered Brian as the girls approached.

"No! You can't make us," said Jillian.

The boys went back to their fishing and ignored the two girls, who kept on walking. Then Francesco impatiently whispered to Brian, "They're on the other side. Quick, get the rock! I want to see it again." They had seen many shale rocks before, but not one like this.

"Let's leave it there for now," Brian said. "We'll come back and get it after supper. Then we'll decide what to do with it."

Francesco agreed. They picked up their fishing gear and headed back.

When their paths parted, and Francesco was riding home, he thought, *I want that fossil. I saw it first. It's mine and I'm not sharing it with Brian.* He immediately turned around, rode back, picked up the rock, and put it in his pocket. He felt good riding home.

Brian could hardly eat his supper, thinking, *"Why couldn't I have found it? I want it for myself. I'm going back for it before Francesco does."* After supper, he rushed out, got on his bike, began to peddle faster, and looked around to see if Francesco was in sight. His front tire hit a large stone and he lost control, toppled over and fell, badly scraping his right arm and knee on the pavement. Driven by the fossil, he got up and, ignoring the pain, kept riding.

Arriving at the spot ten minutes before his friend, Brian frantically looked around. *Where was it?* He searched and searched, but the fossil wasn't there. He knew the girls didn't take it; they were too far away to see it. *It's gone! Darn, did Francesco beat me to it?* he thought angrily. *If he did . . . he's not getting away with it. Just wait 'till he comes.* With torn pants, two scraped-up knees, and a bleeding right elbow, he sat nervously waiting for Francesco.

As soon as Brian saw his buddy riding up the path, he shouted, "You took the fossil! We made a deal, but you just had to have it. YOU STOLE IT!"

Francesco couldn't look at him for guilt. He had betrayed his best friend. They had agreed to share the fossil. "So what," he said, sounding sheepish. "I found it . . . it's mine! I knew you were going to come back for it."

Yelling at each other, the two were soon out of control. Francesco gave Brian a hard shove. Brian tripped, stumbled over some rocks, and then fell backwards into the quarry, landing with a big splash.

Francesco froze in horror. He could not believe what had happened. Getting a grip on himself, he ran to the edge of the bank. He couldn't see Brian. *C'mon Brian, you're a good swimmer! Why aren't you coming up? He must have bumped his head.* At that thought, he dived into the quarry and soon was struggling to grab Brian's arms in the water. He quickly gripped a wrist and pulled him up to the surface. Swimming and panting over to the bank, the two rested there, then gripped the rock wall, and climbed up out of the water.

Coughing and catching their breaths, they sat without talking, unable to look at each other. Then their eyes met, and they suddenly broke into laughter. Francesco took the fossil from his pocket and handed it to Brian. After staring at it a few seconds, Brian handed it back, saying, "Na, it's yours. You found it."

Francesco looked at the rock and said, "C'mon, let's take it to class together. We'll win that rock project."

A shout from the road startled them. "Don't you guys know there's no swimming in the quarry?!" yelled Tamika.

Francesco grinned and yelled, "Buzz off!"

"Quit following us around!" Brian shouted.

The two boys headed home, agreeing on revising their rock project, and realizing their genuine treasure was with each other.

Cooking Camp Adventure

Do what you can, with what you have, where you are.

—THEODORE ROOSEVELT

THE FIRST WEEK OF summer holiday was always a problem for me. Mom would make me join Sport's Camp. This time, I put my foot down.

"I'm not joining sports camp this year! I'm tired of putting up with Eddie Flake and Rudy Pank. They boss me around and call me Pudgy."

I wasn't the fattest boy in camp; the coach's son was much fatter than me—but no one picked on him. After I kicked up such a fuss about it, Mom decided to sign me up at Sports Nutrition Cooking Camp at the community college in town.

"It teaches about cooking healthy food," she told me.

Healthy food? Yuck! Just thinking about celery and brown bread made me want to throw up.

"Hey Mom, I want to join too," my brother interrupted.

That was going to be a problem, because I hated my brother hanging around me!

"Hey Mattie, you'll lose some of your belly fat." My brother was always on my case about losing weight. He always snitched on me when I sneaked some Oreo cookies from the cookie jar.

I couldn't sleep that night for thinking about how I could get out of cooking class! I could pretend to get a stomachache every morning—but mom always knows when I was faking it. Then I figured cooking school would be better than putting up with Eddie and Rudy. Maybe I should just give it a try.

Suddenly I panicked. What would I do if Eli Klim found out I was going to cooking camp? I'd be the wimpiest kid in class. He'd tease me that it was "girlie"—he bullied everyone. One time he picked on me because I was eating a salami sandwich and he said I stunk like a sausage. I had a fight with my mom about never putting salami in my lunch again. I finally fell asleep.

In the morning, Mom handed us each an apron and said, "You'll need to wear it."

"Awww c'mon, Mom, I'm going to look stupid." I got desperate and gave her two sad teary eyes, but it didn't make a difference.

In the car, I tried to think of a way out of wearing that apron. I began to crumple it up and tried stuffing it in my pocket, but it wouldn't fit. I'd just tell the teacher I forgot it. Maybe putting up with Eddie and Rudy was easier than cooking camp.

When I opened the classroom door, I saw a real kitchen with lots of sinks, cupboards, and stoves. Two huge wooden blocks with stools stood on each side of the room, where we worked. A big table set with placemats was at the back of the room. A large, shiny counter for the teacher was in the front.

Six girls and four boys entered. I felt lucky because none of them were from my school. Then this short, stout man walked in.

"Hello. I'm Chef Tino. I'm going to teach you all about nutritious food and how to cook it." He wore a tall white hat and a white shirt and pants. I figured he had to be really brave teaching kids how to cook. Then he put us in groups. I was glad I wasn't with my brother—that way he couldn't snitch on me if I messed up—but I got stuck in a group with three girls. I knew I was headed for trouble. Then I thought that being the only boy in the group meant I could boss them around.

It took Chef Tino over an hour just to go over the rules—like putting long hair up when cooking, and not wearing open-toe shoes. He was thinking about the girls for those rules. He said, "We have to wash our hands before we touch the food and wash them again after we touch the food." Cripes! I was going to be the only one of all my friends with clean-looking hands.

"Aprons must be worn," he insisted. Now I was doomed! "These hats must be worn at all times while cooking! They are called a 'toque.' Be proud of them; they say you are an expert." He handed us each a toque, just like his. Gosh! We all looked rather silly with them on.

"I'm going to keep a close watch on all of you to pick the Junior Chef for the week. The winner becomes my assistant chef. I'm looking for the student who does things the proper way—Chef Tino's way," he said. I glanced at my brother and saw a big smile on his face. I knew he was thinking he would be the winner.

"It's time to start cooking! We are going to make an omelet today."

I didn't know why he picked an omelet. Eggs weren't really one of my favorite foods. I thought hamburgers would have made a much better choice.

"Eggs contain lots of protein," Chef added, as he held one up before us.

Who cares about protein? It's cracking those eggs I was getting worried about! First, he made us wash our hands with soap, and then he gave us each two eggs.

"Tap them on the table," he said, "then break them over the bowl. Be careful that pieces of the shells don't fall into the bowl."

As I looked around, I saw everyone, including my brother, trying to pick the little shell pieces out with a fork.

Lucy, one of the girls in my group, was telling me how I was doing it all wrong. Girls always think they know everything! At least I got mine to drop in the bowl—one of her eggs landed on the floor beside her feet. Chef Tino didn't look very happy; he made her clean up the mess.

Golly, he didn't even yell at her, but her face turned beet red. I judged her a little too quickly. I noticed it wasn't so bad being in her group, just in case I did something stupid too.

Next, Chef Tino showed us how to chop these long, hollow, onion-flavored leaves called chives. "Chop them fine using a small knife on the cutting board, and then add them to the eggs," Chef Tino ordered.

Just as he told us to be careful not to cut our fingers, Lucy let out a scream. Wow, blood was oozing out of her finger! Chef Tino ran to get the first aid kit. All the kids scrambled around our table to see what the commotion was about. This time Lucy was as pale as a ghost. By now Chef Tino didn't seem too impressed with her; she was kind of giving him a hard time.

"Now, measure one tablespoon of water and add it to the mixture," he continued. Gee, it's really hard to measure one tablespoon without spilling it.

"Add some salt and pepper, and—gently—mix it all."

Everyone was banging forks against the glass bowls. It was getting louder and louder 'till finally Chef shouted "Stop!" The room became silent!

He handed us each a small frying pan and some butter to heat. "Be careful to keep your hands away from the burners," he demanded.

Suddenly we heard my brother, Josh, yell "Ouch!" Yeah, he got burned. It's a good thing Chef Tino still had the first aid kit handy. Cooking can be dangerous!

"After the butter melts, pour the egg mixture into the pan. As soon as the mixture gets firm, gently loosen the omelet with the spatula and fold the eggs over," he explained.

Simple? Not to the girls in my group. I was surprised when Chef Tino told me to help them. I knew they weren't too happy about that. When it comes to cooking, girls think they know it all!

"Then slide it out onto your plate," he said, showing us how.

Presto! It was ready to eat. We all took our omelets and gathered at the large table in the back to enjoy them. They were good! You can always get a fine meal learning how to cook!

"Clean up your area and wash your hands," he bellowed when we finished eating. In my opinion, that was the worst part of the class.

"It's time to choose the Junior Chef of the day," he announced. Everyone sat nervously waiting, looking at each other, then at Chef Tino.

"The Junior Chef of the day goes to . . . Mattie Brown, for being a master chef, helping his group, and following instructions the correct way." He handed me an apron that had JUNIOR CHEF written on it. Everyone clapped!

I was shocked! I looked over at my brother and saw that he didn't look very happy and I knew he was disappointed he wasn't picked.

For the first time ever, I knew what it felt like to be the most popular kid in the class. It actually turned out to be fun. I couldn't wait to see what tomorrow's adventure was going to be like!

"See you in the morning!" Chef Tino yelled, nodding to us as we shuffled out the door.

"For sure!" I shouted back, winked at the girls, and picked up my apron with a smile. It was going to be a great week after all. Good ole Mom!

Clownin' with Bobo

Those who bring sunshine to the lives of others
cannot keep it from themselves.

—Sir James Matthew Barrie

"Stephanie, hurry, I can hear it starting now!" Tyler yelled as they raced with their bikes to the park, arriving while the mayor announced the town's festival events.

"The spaghetti-eating contest will begin at the picnic tables, and our surprise guest will perform at two o'clock at the pavilion."

"Hey Stephanie, are you going to enter the spaghetti-eating contest"?

"Are you kidding? No one can beat Eli. He *always* wins."

"Yeah, let's get an ice cream."

As they passed the pavilion, they noticed someone strange walking behind the spectator area.

"Tyler, did you see that"?

"What was it"?

"It looked like a clown."

Suddenly, they stood facing the clown, who was blowing up balloons with a little pump.

"Hello kids! Have a balloon."

Surprisingly, Tyler began to stutter, "Uh, uh . . . are you a real clown?"

"Yep, I'm Bobo! What's your name?"

"I'm Tyler and she's Stephanie. Are you doing the show?"

"In forty-five minutes. I'm blowing up balloons for the kids today. Can you two give me a hand? I'm running late."

"Sure."

"Stephanie, you hand me the balloons, and Tyler, you put them in that bin after they're pumped up."

The two gazed at the clown in admiration. Then Tyler asked, "Hey Bob, how did you get to be a clown?"

"My neighbors, Klinker and Sparkle, were clowns; they inspired me. I saw them perform here, at this event many years ago. When I saw the little children laughing and having fun, I thought, 'I want to do that too.'"

"Wow! How old were you?" asked Tyler.

"Twelve! Klinker and Sparkle ran a ten-week class at their house. They taught us the history of clowns, basic makeup, tricks like how to make these balloon animals, and ideas on how to perform as clowns."

"A clown school?" Stephanie interrupted.

"Oh, yes! You can't be a clown without knowing anything. Did you know that clowns are also called 'Joeys'? The name comes from a famous seventeenth-century Italian clown named Joseph Grimaldi. He was a pantomime clown. He acted the character of a fool, and introduced audience participation. That's pretty much what I do."

Stephanie was staring at the clown's funny face, and asked, "Did they teach you how to paint your face too?"

"You bet! I am a *whiteface* clown because I use white makeup to cover my entire face and neck. I paint my eyebrows with special black paint and red for the mouth. We are also performance clowns; we put on a show. I do tricks, sing, and create balloon animals—that sort of stuff.

Whereas character clowns take on personalities—like a hobo. Their makeup and costume match the character they are acting."

"The gag clowns do funny tricks. They'll use squirt guns and bicycle horns, and ride tricycles, performing in groups of three in a circus."

"That's cool! Clowns get to do anything just to make people laugh."

"Not really anything, Tyler. Clowns follow rules also, like no drinking alcohol, no smoking, and no name-calling. We make the children feel comfortable."

"Where did you get your funny costume?" Tyler was admiring Bobo's orange, yellow, and red frizzy wig.

"After graduating from clown school, I went to The Party Shop. I got a red rubber nose, this wig, and a funny straw hat. I wore pajamas with blue polka dots, and red pom-poms. That was my first costume, and I still have it."

"I bet you were a big hit in school," Stephanie said enviously.

"Oh, no! Some kids in my class bullied me because I was a clown. They made fun of me, and that really made me feel sad. They never wanted me as their friend. But then I met two really nice kids, who accepted me as I was."

"I know what that's like; sometimes Stephanie and I get bullied because we're friends and ride our bikes together, but we don't care," Tyler said.

"I wasn't going to change my attitude either," Bobo continued, "not for anyone. I am who I am. If I can make one person smile—make a difference for one person—then my job as a clown is worth it, and I'm very happy doing it."

"When I got to high school, lots of kids wanted to be my friend. I was quite popular; I was nicknamed 'Bo,' which made me really feel good."

Placing the last balloon in the bin, Stephanie noticed the time. "It's almost two, Tyler; we won't get a seat. See you at the show, Bobo."

"Thanks for helping," Bobo smiled back.

As Tyler and Stephanie turned away, Bobo had an idea. "Hey you two, how about helping me on the show?"

"Really . . . Doing what?"

"You can be my assistants, handing out balloons while I make their balloon animals."

"Sure, okay!" they shouted.

Bobo had made two kids extra happy that day. That's what a clown's job is all about!

Charlie

The love we give away is the only love we keep.

—UNKNOWN

I WAS HAVING A pretty decent life until my Dad broke the news that we were moving to the city.

"I'm not going anywhere. I'm staying right here on our farm." But no matter how much I complained, it wasn't going to make any difference.

I pleaded with my Mom, but she was not cooperative at all. When grown-ups make up their mind, not even a kid can change it.

"You'll enjoy living in the city, Isabella. You won't have as many chores, and you'll be able to walk to school instead of taking the bus," Mom said.

"I don't mind riding on the bus, and I love doing my chores, especially feeding our chickens and pigs. What about Charlie? We won't be able to bring him to the city."

I couldn't sleep that night, thinking about moving to the city and leaving behind my pet pig, Charlie. I had to take desperate measures and come up with some kind of a plan that would make my Mom and Dad change their minds. I could run away, but that wouldn't work, because Mom would call the police and then the whole community would be out looking for me. I tried my big tears to make them feel guilty, but that didn't work either. They just ignored me.

"Isabella," I heard my mom calling. "I spoke to the clerk at city hall and they told me that you will be allowed to bring Charlie, but he is to be of no problem to the neighbors. If they complain, you will have to give him up. Is it a deal?"

"You bet." I quickly ran off to see Charlie. "Hey Charlie, you're coming to the city with us." Charlie licked my face. We were both excited.

Seeing Charlie's pen in the back of our new house in the city was awesome. I think he felt a little uncomfortable at first. He was squealing around quite a bit, but he finally settled down when I brought him some apples.

I couldn't wait to run home after school to take Charlie for a walk.

"Isabella, make sure you put the leash on him. He's not familiar with the area," Mom remarked.

As I walked down to the park, I saw Nicholas, one of my new friends from school.

"Isabella, what are you doing with that pig?" he hollered.

"Hi Nicholas, this is my pet pig, Charlie. We are going for a walk to the park. Pigs make great pets; they are very playful and loving animals too," I explained.

Two joggers stopped right in front of Charlie, looking at him funnily. "Hey, is that a real pig that I see? Did he run away from a farm?" The girl and her friend both laughed.

"Come on Charlie, let's go home; city people aren't very nice," I sighed.

I talked to Mom about what happened, and she said, "City people aren't used to seeing pets other than cats and dogs. Why don't we walk Charlie to school tomorrow, and we can introduce Charlie to the kids. Then I'll take him home when the bell rings." I thought it would be worth a try. Charlie kept squealing all night.

"Isabella, go out in the back and simmer Charlie down; he is disturbing the neighbors," my Dad hollered. After calming him down with a few pears, we all fell asleep.

In the morning, Mom was waiting for me to get Charlie. As soon as we walked up to the fence of the school, all the children peeled out laughing. Just then the bell rang.

I guess that noise was too much for Charlie; he started to squeal very loudly. He darted in circles until he jerked the leash out of Mom's hand. Suddenly he quickly scurried into the big doors of the school, following all the children.

"Isabella, run after Charlie!" Mom shouted.

I ran into the school and saw him squealing down the hallway. Then I thought of a plan. I ran into my classroom and yelled, "Charlie, over here!" He dashed past me inside the room. By now all the children were blaring out laughing.

All that noise offended Charlie. He was running like crazy. He tore all over the place, bumping into tables and chairs, scattering books and papers everywhere, squealing and snorting. The whole room went wild, and I couldn't catch up to him. Miss Bailey yelled for everyone to get out into the hall. She slammed the door and told me to catch Charlie. As I was running to grab him, he bumped into the large globe on the stand, which tumbled down to the floor. I snatched Charlie just as he was headed towards the aquarium. Mom made her way into the classroom and put the leash on Charlie. She apologized to everyone. The children were still laughing at me and Charlie. It made me sad.

That night I got more bad news from Dad. He told me that Charlie couldn't stay with us anymore because the neighbors in our subdivision complained about his squealing.

I cried myself to sleep that night. I couldn't go with Dad back to the farm to return Charlie. I lost my best friend.

The next day, when Dad came home from work, I saw him coming out of the car carrying a big brown box.

"Isabella," he called, "open the box."

As I opened the lid, inside was a beautiful little golden lab puppy.

"I think this pet will be acceptable for you, your friends, and the neighbors."

"Oh, yes," I laughed.

He might never take the place of Charlie, but he was the most adorable puppy I had ever seen. As he grew, he had a good strong bark, so I couldn't figure out why his barking never bothered the neighbors. Oh, by the way, his name is Charlie too!

Flight into Danger

The secret of happiness is not to do what you like, but to like what you do.

—UNKNOWN

THE DAY MY DAD got a job at Niagara Helicopter, Fly and Dine, changed both our lives. He thinks *he* got the lucky break becoming head chef at their restaurant, but actually, I'm the one who came out shining.

It's an interesting business. Tourists make reservations, arrive, order lunch or dinner, then tour Niagara Falls by helicopter. By the time they fly back, their food is ready.

It all started when Dad came home from work, and he bellowed, "Guess what? All employees received free passes for family and friends. Tomorrow we're taking a free helicopter tour of Niagara Falls."

It was like a genie appeared to grant kids their ultimate wish. My sister and I mobbed Dad to see the passes. Mom wasn't interested—she hates flying. It makes her nauseous and she's terrified of heights. She's kind of wimpy that way.

I couldn't sleep that night, tossing and turning, for thinking of the things that could happen on that ride. I finally dozed off after 2 a.m.

In the morning Mom drove my sister and me to the restaurant to meet Dad. He looked cool in his chef's outfit—I loved the hat—and I was impressed by how clean and fancy everything looked. The restaurant had ceiling-to-floor windows so customers could view the helicopter take off and land on the big pad around the terminal.

Stephanie and I ordered the Hamburger Deluxe dinner, and Mom had grilled chicken salad with the soup of the day, all recommended by Dad of course. As soon as we placed our order, a lady in a blue suit came to collect our passes.

"You can go first, Tyler," said my sister, Stephanie, sounding a little scared. "I'll go on the next ride."

The idea of not going on with my sister gave me a feeling of independence. She surprised me since she usually wants to be first at everything. Not this time; helicopter rides must be a little scary for girls.

Five tourists were in line behind me. The lady took our passes, and directed us through the back door, saying, "The helicopter will land soon. The pilot will tell you when to embark."

We all stood eagerly waiting. Within minutes, the sound of the helicopter became louder and louder, as it come closer. As it was landing, I got goose bumps watching it. Those rotors were awesome! The wind from them got stronger and the noise became horrendous. I was anticipating the ride of my life!

The helicopter rotors slowed down to where you could see them. What an amazing sight! It was metallic blue and silver with rainbow stripes down the side. The door opened and six passengers got out. The pilot then directed us to get on. My crafty plan was to let the others go ahead so that I could sit next to the pilot—and it worked! This was going to be my luckiest day ever!

"Good afternoon, ladies and gentlemen. I'm your pilot, Jacob Dunn. Please fasten your seatbelt as we are ready for takeoff." Then he turned to me, asking, "Are you ready?"

"Oh yeah," I said. The fact that he actually talked to me personally made me feel special, like a little kid, even though I was the tight end on the football team.

All the buttons, switches, and gadgets along the front panel looked cool. When all our seatbelts were secure, he showed us where the parachutes were in case of emergency. With one push of a panel button, the rotors increased speed. All the panel lights lit up as the pilot pulled the throttle to lift, while the GPS monitor showed the exact position of the helicopter. I was amazed! I watched the altitude climbing from sixty meters to two hundred and then it held its height at three hundred meters. The big windows of the helicopter gave a spectacular and beautiful panoramic view of the city and the falls.

"What's your name?" the pilot asked.

"Tyler—Tyler Jennings," I said proudly.

Pointing to the different buttons and gadgets, the pilot explained, "Tyler, the top rotors lift the aircraft; the rotors on the tail give the helicopter its push and direction." I couldn't believe the attention he gave me, like I was someone important! Then he announced, "Everyone, please put your headsets on for the audio tour and select your preferred language."

Below us, the city was drawn into neat sections of houses, streets, and roads. The tall buildings peered right at me. It was scary. I clutched my hands between my knees, hoping no one could see I was nervous. The voice on the audio was explaining the tour while we gazed at the re-markable view.

We crossed over the Whirlpool Rapids, and the Rain-bow Bridge, which connects Canada to the United States. Then we flew over the American Falls and trailed towards the Skylon Tower. As the helicopter followed the Niagara River over the Horseshoe Falls, we could see the gorge down below, and then we hovered in a stationary position as we all admired the astounding scene. It was absolutely incredible; rainbows appeared and disappeared from all directions. Mists of water like smoke rose up from the falls. The whole scene was spectacular!

The voice on the audio explained, "The name Niagara Falls originates from an Iroquois word meaning "thunder of waters." It was formed when glaciers receded from the Wisconsin Glaciation, during the last ice age, about ten thousand years ago. More than six million cubic feet of wa-ter pours over every minute. Erosion over time has caused the falls to recede approximately eleven kilometers and has changed the shape of Horseshoe Falls from a small arch to a horseshoe bend. Niagara Falls is known for its beauty and as a source of hydroelectric power."

Suddenly everyone was yelling and pointing out the window. "Down there! There's a man in the gorge."

I looked and saw him—a dark spot in the water! The pilot immediately radioed in, but with all the commotion in the cabin, I couldn't hear him talking.

Looking at me, he shouted, "We have a person in dis-tress! We have to do an emergency rescue because of our proximity to the victim. I need someone to go down and grab him before the current takes him down. You're young and strong. You have to help me, Tyler. We do not have time to waste."

Oh my God—was he asking me to do the rescuing? I wanted to yell "No way!" But I got a grip on myself and said, "Okay, tell me what to do." I couldn't believe I just said that! Was I crazy? But the guy down there needed help. I didn't have much of a choice.

The pilot explained on the PA, "We have to do an emergency rescue before the current takes him down. Quiet down and keep your seat belts on."

Turning to me again, he said, "Tyler, have you ever been on a bungee cord?"

"Uh, yeah," I replied, "at Canada's Wonderland."

"Good. This strong cable cord is very similar, only it is not elastic. It will not spring back. The winch will take you down. There is a harness with a seat for you and another harness placed around your chest for the other person. When you get down there, extend your arms to the man. I will lower the helicopter as low as I can. Any questions?"

Any questions? You've gotta be kidding, dude! But I said I'd do it and I would. I decided not to think about it. I needed to think about the guy down there and do it!

As quick as I could, I harnessed myself in. My hands and knees wouldn't stop shaking. By now the helicopter was down close to fifty meters from the gorge, hovering directly over the victim. The pilot opened the emergency door of the helicopter—and l jumped and felt the cable hold me and then lower. All I could see was a mass of mist and water, swirling around. Then the man became visible; he was trying to stay above the water. A rush of adrenaline shot through me—but it seemed like I was watching someone else. I heard myself begging, "Please God, help me!"

I knew I could do this. My feet were almost touching the water and became soaked. I bent over and reached out to him. After struggling for several seconds, our hands finally clasped. He had the good sense to grip the cable with the other hand and pull himself up to my chest. The rest came easy; I harnessed him in, waved to the pilot, and we went back up!

Everyone clapped when we got back onboard the helicopter. One of the passengers unharnessed us and helped us lay down. Another handed me a blanket. An ambulance was waiting for him when we landed. My knees finally stopped shaking.

When I got off the helicopter, I got the shock of my life! TV cameras were already there, and a lot of news people crowded around, yelling questions at me about the rescue, like I was some superstar.

I told them all, "I just followed the pilot's instructions."

"Hey, I'm starved! Let's get that hamburger that's waiting for us," I said, turning away.

"Great idea," my dad said.

"He needs to get dry!" Mom shouted, pushing them away.

As we all walked back into the restaurant, I gave a final glance at the news press buzzing around. I thought, *Today I had a taste of what it's like to be famous!*

Isabella and the Butterfly

Where there is great love, there are always miracles.

—WILLA CATHER

ISABELLA LIVED IN A little village in Italy. Every day after school, Isabella would go to her favorite place behind her house and play. Yellow daisies and white baby's breath covered her back yard. Orange- and black-colored butterflies fluttered all about her and hovered from flower to flower. Sometimes they would rest on her arms and cheeks, tickling her like soft feathers. Isabella would pretend that she was the butterfly queen, soaring from flower to flower. She would spread her arms and pretend they were huge wings that carried her far up into the sky.

Furry rabbits with bushy tails scampered about Isabella's feet. Little brown squirrels would rush up to Isabella and eat the nuts that she gathered off the palm of her hand. Beautiful birds chirped in the branches of the tall trees.

Huge snow-capped mountains towered through the fluffy clouds that surrounded this small village. She imagined that the mountains were huge castles and she was the princess of her village, ruling over the sun and earth.

"I am the queen of the kingdom," she hollered as her voice echoed back. It was a beautiful, magical place for her where she was able to laugh and feel happy. When she felt sad, she would go there, and her sadness would go away.

One day while Isabella was feeding the squirrels in her back yard, she found a cocoon on a small branch that fell on the ground. *I will bring it to school and show my teacher*, she thought.

"We will put the cocoon in a jar. It is spring, and the cocoon will soon open up and turn into a beautiful butterfly," her teacher explained.

At school, Isabella drew a picture of her house below the mountains, with her favorite orange butterfly sitting on a white daisy among the grass with the furry animals all around her.

"Isabella, your picture is very beautiful. Your parents will be proud of you," said her teacher.

When she got home her mother said, "I have some good news, Isabella." She decided to keep her picture behind her back. She thought, *I will show it to them after the special news*.

Her mother looked at her and said, "Isabella, do you remember Zia Anna from Canada? She wants us to live with her! We will be moving to Canada soon."

Isabella put her head down. "That would be nice." But deep in her heart, Isabella was sad. She slowly walked away, trying not to cry.

"I do not want to leave my house in Italy," she sighed. I want to stay here with all my friends. Suddenly, her picture was not important anymore. She placed it on the table and ran to her favorite place, sat on a little grassy hill, and cried.

A big orange butterfly landed on her arm. Her big teardrops fell on its wings. A little furry squirrel scampered around her and a bird was chirping a happy tune. But she paid no attention to them. Nothing could make Isabella happy.

I wonder if there are any beautiful butterflies, or furry squirrels, or big snow-capped mountains in Canada? she thought. Suddenly her enchanted place lost all its magic.

She went to bed that night very sad.

"It will be a much better life for us in Canada," her mother explained. But Isabella could not imagine living without her friends and her beautiful house in Italy.

"Come and play with us, Isabella," her friends called to her at school the next day, but she was too sad to play.

"What is the matter, Isabella?" asked her teacher. "Why are you so sad?"

"We will be moving to Canada. I do not want to leave my house and all my friends here."

Suddenly the cocoon in the jar on the shelf started to open.

"Look at Isabella's cocoon!" the children shouted. A beautiful orange butterfly was emerging. Its delicate wings were struggling to get out. Finally, the wings began to expand and become firm to support the body, and then the butterfly found its way out of the cocoon.

Just as the teacher opened the lid, the butterfly fluttered about, and landed on Isabella's arm.

Isabella thought about what the teacher had said as she looked at the new butterfly that had appeared from the cocoon. Leaving the old cocoon behind, the butterfly fluttered about.

After school she ran home and went to her favorite magical place. She picked a daisy and placed it in her hair. An orange and black butterfly rested on the daisy and then fluttered onto her hand. "I will be just like you when I move to Canada. I will leave and have a new home, and new friends."

She wanted to be just like these butterflies. She was now ready to accept the new experiences and adventures that moving to a new country would bring. *I will be happy to live with my Zia Anna's family in Canada*, she thought.

A calm and cheerful feeling filled Isabella's heart. She was no longer afraid to move to Canada. She welcomed the changes that would come about in her life as she watched the butterfly flutter far away in the distance.

With a smile on her face, she knew that the beautiful butterflies would also be waiting for her in Canada.

The Magic Carousel

The best and most beautiful things in the world cannot be seen or touched but are felt in the heart.

—UNKNOWN

FRANCESCO CLUTCHED HIS MOTHER'S hand as they walked the midway at the fairgrounds. There were so many things to see that he didn't know where to look first. With every step they took, someone new was shouting, inviting them to enter their tent, play their game, or buy their food.

A funny clown selling balloons handed Francesco a big red one. Smiling with approval, his mom handed the clown some coins.

"Hang on to your balloon or it will float high in the sky," warned the clown. Francesco was too excited to listen to what the clown said.

A few steps further on, Francesco noticed a large carousel with a big sign that said:

RIDE THE MAGICAL MERRY-GO-ROUND
Find the magic horse!

"Mom, it looks just like the wind-up merry-go-round Grandma gave me. Even the horses are the same colors. I want to go on it, please." He nearly burst with excitement when he heard her shout, "One ticket please!" As he stepped up onto the wooden floor, he felt as if he had entered his musical carousel.

"Which horse do you want, sonny?" asked the ticket man.

Francesco pointed to the brown Shetland pony.

The man lifted Francesco with his rugged hands, put him on the saddle, and whispered in his ear, "Good choice! Grab the reins. Hang on tight. Believe with your heart and listen to the music." He winked at Francesco with his caring eyes, and then turned away.

As Francesco grabbed the leather reins over the horse's neck, his big red balloon slipped out of his hand, and sailed up into the sky. Francesco was so thrilled to be on the carousel that he paid no attention to the balloon. Sitting high on the horse, he felt a magical tingling throughout his body.

Could this be the magic horse? he wondered.

He saw his mother waving at him.

"Mom, look at me!" he shouted and waved back. It seemed like he waited forever for the carousel to move.

Suddenly, the music grew louder, and the carousel started turning slowly. Then it began to whirl quickly, round and round. The horses were moving up and down! Francesco was excited and giggling while he was spinning faster and faster. Then an amazing thing happened! With a jerk, the horse's pole suddenly detached from the carousel and, within that magical moment, the little pony was galloping in time to the enchanted music high up into the fluffy clouds.

Francesco could not believe this was happening! It seemed as if the horse was running an exciting race in midair. A warm wind brushed against his face, blowing his hair all about. The pony's mane bounced up and down like small wings as it galloped higher and higher. Shouting with laughter, Francesco was entering the magical world of make-believe!

Everything was spinning as the pony pranced through the sky. Looking up, he saw his red balloon sailing overhead. Wow! Flocks of white seagulls glided straight at him. He quickly ducked and the gulls curved away, just missing him. Fierce black eagles were aiming at him. Francesco dodged as they swooped under the pony. He looked down and suddenly he became afraid. His great adventure was becoming dangerous! Now he was frightened. It was all so incredible; the magic seemed powerful and endless!

He wanted to return to the carousel. Not knowing how to get back, he panicked. What could he do? *I'll shut my eyes*, he thought, *and wish very hard for the pony to take me back.*

He wished with all his heart, but he was still flying. So he whispered into the pony's ear, "Take me back to the merry-go-round. Take me back to the merry-go-round," but he was still in the sky.

Desperate, he finally remembered the ticket man's words, "Listen to the music."

That's it, he thought, *the music! I need to listen to the magical music!*

As he closed his eyes and listened to the faint music far away, Francesco felt his pony slowing down, and flying lower. The carousel was getting closer . . . closer . . . moving into the right space on the carousel . . . and with a quick snap, the pony's pole reattached! Francesco gave a sigh of relief. Looking around, he was happy to see his mother waiting.

The merry-go-round slowed, and then stopped with a jolt. As the tall man came over to help Francesco off the pony, he winked and said, "Welcome back."

"Thank you," said Francesco. "They'll never believe me, will they?"

"No," said the ticket man, smiling, "but it's yours to cherish always."

Marathon in Space

Believe you can and you're halfway there.

—THEODORE ROOSEVELT

HAVE YOU EVER TRIED to do the impossible, like twitching your nose and making anything you want to happen? Or pointing a finger at an object and making it move without touching it? Have you ever wanted to fulfill a dream, like finding a cure for cancer? How about running the Boston Marathon in outer space?

Approximately two hundred miles above the Earth, female astronaut Sunita Williams performed the impossible and attempted something no other astronaut had ever accomplished. As the space shuttle orbited around the Earth, simultaneously, Sunita ran the Boston Marathon.

Why would any astronaut want to run the marathon in a shuttle during a space flight? Perhaps knowing the environment inside the shuttle will help us to understand why astronaut Sunita wanted to attempt the run.

SHUTTLE LIFE

Shuttle life is exciting, as well as challenging, and scientists try to make the crew members stay fairly comfortable. The air is about 79 percent nitrogen and 21 percent oxygen. It is cleaner than Earth's air and pollen free. The temperature is kept about 75 degrees Fahrenheit, and carbon dioxide and other impurities are removed by filters. Within the shuttle, the crew wears ordinary clothing, so that they are able to move about, work, and relax without the interference of a bulky spacesuit, which is worn when an astronaut is working outside the space shuttle.

Meals are eaten on a regular basis and are mainly dehydrated because there are no refrigerators in the shuttle. This also saves weight and storage.

Sanitation is a priority within the shuttle, as it is in your own home on Earth; therefore, all living areas are cleaned regularly. Eating utensils are cleaned with wet wipes containing strong disinfectant. Sponge baths are taken by crew members every other day. Toilets much like the one in an airplane are used in the shuttle. Sounds quite normal, doesn't it!

Physical exercise is important for maintaining a healthy lifestyle on Earth. The same applies during a space flight in the shuttle. Exercise helps prevent certain diseases such as high blood pressure and strengthens the cardiovascular system. Regular exercising also increases bone density and joint mobility and strengthens the immune system. Although it seems like it would be fun living in an environment with no gravity, it does have undesirable effects. Crew members follow planned exercise programs to counteract *microgravity's* effect on the heart, veins, bones, and muscles. Doctors believe that it is important for astronauts to exercise regularly while orbiting in space because of microgravity's side effects.

MICROGRAVITY

Microgravity is a force of gravity so low that weightlessness occurs. While in space, astronauts don't use their legs to walk around. They don't need the bones and muscles to hold them up as they would under the force of gravity; unfortunately, prolonged exposure to microgravity causes changes in the human body, including bone loss and impaired muscle movement and blood circulation. As a result, there are specific challenges to staying healthy while in space. That is why Sunita Williams wanted to make fitness a priority during her expedition. Her intent was to educate everyone about being physically fit in general.

Gravity is everywhere, but it is not felt in an orbiting spacecraft. Objects and people appear to be floating although they still maintain the same mass. Outside a spacecraft, astronauts performing space walks can move large objects, such as the Hubble Space Telescope. Devices such as foot restraints, ropes, and chains must be used so that they will not float away while they work. The most common problem experienced by astronauts in the initial hours of microgravity is known as Space Adaptation Syndrome (SAS), commonly referred to as space sickness. Symptoms include nausea, vomiting, headaches, and tiredness. The duration of space sickness varies, but has never lasted more than three days; after that, the body adjusts to the new environment.

RUNNING THE MARATHON

Sunita Williams, a skillful runner, was training for the marathon for months while serving a six-month period as a flight engineer aboard the International Space Station (ISS). She ran at least four times a week; two longer runs and two shorter runs. Sunita qualified for the Boston Marathon when she ran in the Houston Marathon previously. But her biggest challenge was how to run in a *microgravity* environment. Scientists came up with a perfect solution: a specially designed TVIS treadmill (Treadmill Vibration Isolation System) with bungee cords connecting the user to the treadmill . This specific treadmill will not vibrate in a microgravity environment, which is important since delicate science experiments are often being performed in nearby labs within the space shuttle. Running on the TVIS treadmill can be uncomfortable because the harness puts a strain on the runner's hips and shoulders. Staying harnessed to the treadmill would be Sunita's greatest difficulty while completing the run. However, she endured the hardships involved in the run.

The Boston Athletic Association had issued Sunita bib number 14000. The bib had been sent electronically to NASA (the National Aeronautics and Space Administration), which in turn forwarded it to her. Sunita's plan was to encourage children to start making physical fitness part of their daily lives. On April 16, 2007, she was the first astronaut to run the marathon in orbit.

Sunita Williams orbited the Earth twice while running as fast as eight miles per hour. At the same time, she was flying more than five miles each second as she completed the Boston Marathon on the specially designed treadmill. Her official completion time was four hours and twenty-three minutes. Of course, Sunita ran under better weather conditions than her Boston competitors. In Boston, it was 48 degrees with some rain, mist, and wind gusts of twenty-eight miles per hour. The shuttle weather was 78 degrees with no wind or rain and with 50 percent humidity. Her crew members cheered her on and gave her oranges during the race.

A SUPER WOMAN

Sunita Williams was born September 19, 1965, in Uclid, Ohio. She is a United States Naval Officer and a NASA astronaut. She is the second woman of Indian heritage to have been selected by NASA and the second astronaut of Slovene heritage, on her mother's side. Sunita was assigned to the ISS as a member of Expedition 14, and then joined Expedition 15. She holds the record for the longest space flight (195 days) for a female space traveler. As soon as the six crew members aboard the *Atlantis* landed, Sunita was chosen as Person of the Week by the ABC television network.

Sunita Williams's impossible dream came true. With determination and advanced technology, her goal aboard the space shuttle became a reality. So, if your ambition is to accomplish an impossible dream, don't give up. Think about Sunita Williams, who had a dream to run the Boston Marathon while orbiting the Earth, and to exemplify the importance of physical fitness in all facets of life, even aboard the space shuttle *Atlantis*.

A Taste of Honey

Let us think about each other and help each other
to show love and do good deeds.

—HEBREWS 10:24

LARGE FLUFFY SNOWFLAKES TUMBLED silently over the
North Pole, creating a blanket of snow all over Santa's toy
shop. Inside, the elves kept warm and busy, making toys for
all the children in the world. You could hear from as far
away as the reindeers' stables all the machines whirring, the
hammers banging, and the elves singing and whistling as
they worked. Christmas Eve was very near!

Two brown teddy bears, Kody and Kodianne, were
made especially for twins Brian and Brianne. They were
amazed, watching the elves work, while they sat on the shelf
waiting to be delivered. Every day at lunch time, Kody and
Kodianne watched the oldest elf as he climbed the ladder to
the top shelf of the cupboard and brought down a big jar of
honey and a huge basket of cookies to have with their tea.

Oh, how Kody wished to have just a little lick of that
sweet, thick honey and a crumb of the cookies the elves were

enjoying, but he knew it was impossible. Still, he dreamed of it every time the elves ate.

The two bears also watched the elves, from their shelf, take a warm bath every night before going off to bed. They would hear them giggling as they splashed water up to their faces. Now, it happens that every year, on the night before Christmas Eve, something magical overtakes the toy shop. As soon as the clock strikes twelve, while the elves are sound asleep, every toy comes alive! Kody and Kodianne could not believe it when their bodies stood up! Their arms began waving and their legs kicked out. Off the shelf they jumped and danced, hopped, and skipped around the room. Every toy in Santa's toy shop was moving with excitement!

Kody had a brilliant idea! He wanted to taste the honey and crunchy cookies that were up in the cupboard. He nudged Kodianne and said, "Let me stand on your shoulders, so I can get the jar of honey and some cookies."

Kodianne was not certain she should help him, but she wanted a taste also, so up went Kody onto her shoulders. As he was reaching for the jar, he accidentally tipped it! Oh dear, honey poured all down his front! His fur was all sticky and gooey! When Kodianne saw what had happened, she became very upset!

"Now look what you have done, Kody! Santa cannot deliver you to Brian all sticky! What shall we do?"

"I will fill the tub with water and bathe, just like the elves do." He thought it was the only solution to become clean again. Quickly they filled the tub with water. Kody grabbed the bottle of soap and poured some into the water. Like magic, soapsuds covered the tub! He quickly jumped in. Soft bubbles drifted up and floated around the room, landing on his nose, his ears, and his neck! He never felt this way before. Even the elves' rubber ducky quacked with delight! He was having a fantastic time!

The clock was now heading towards six o'clock of Christmas Eve. Kody felt himself getting weaker! Kodianne was getting worried; the magic was nearing its end.

"Hurry, Kody," she called, "all the toys are returning to their shelves!" Kodianne wanted to hurry out, but she decided to turn back and help Kody! She grabbed a towel, wiped the soap off him, and they ran back, reaching the shelf just before the clock struck six! All the magic disappeared—but every toy was back in place! It was silent again in the toy shop.

Santa strolled in shortly, with the elves leaping ahead. They packed all the toys in a huge sack. By evening, they had finished. The big doors slid open and, in a flash, Santa and his sleigh drove out and soared high in the sky. The jingle of the bells could be heard fading off in the distance.

Early Christmas morning, Brian and Brianne rushed from their bedroom down to their Christmas tree. They opened their gifts with excitement! Santa had brought exactly what they wanted, two teddy bears. They hugged their bears as parents hug their children. Suddenly, Brian felt something sticky on the back of his bear's neck. Curious, he rubbed it with his fingers. Oddly enough, it felt and smelled just . . . like . . . honey.

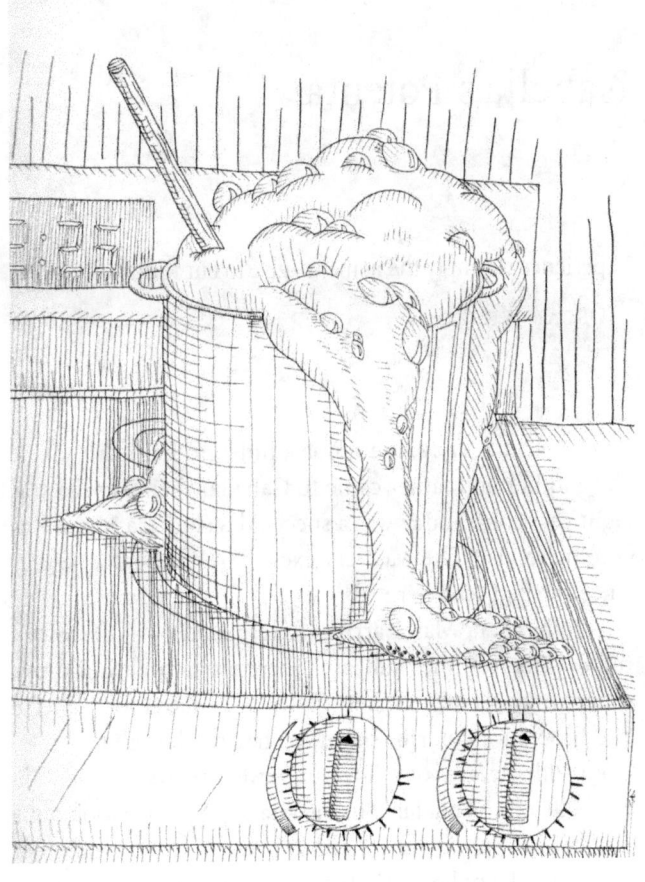

Isabella's Polenta

Experience is simply the name we give to our mistakes.

—OSCAR WILDE

ONCE UPON A TIME, there was a little girl named Isabella. Her mother and father came to Canada when Isabella was eight years old. Today was a special day; her Zia Maria was coming to visit. She was very excited. It had been one year since she had seen her.

When Zia Maria arrived, she pulled out a large bag full of gifts from her suitcase. There was a beautiful dress, different kinds of toys, and pretty pink shoes for Isabella. She brought a colorful shawl for her mother and a table-cloth with pictures of yellow sunflowers all over it, which fit perfectly on the big table in the kitchen. She also took out a large bag of special corn flour to make polenta. In another hefty bag, she pulled out a big round copper pot to cook the polenta. This made Isabella very happy because Zia Maria knew that polenta was Isabella's favorite food.

Every Saturday was Polenta Day. Isabella would help her mother make the polenta. She would take out a large pot and fill it with water. As soon as the water boiled over the stove, they would pour the corn flour into the water. Her mother would let Isabella stir and stir for a long time until the corn flour got thick and gooey, just like porridge. Then her mother would pour the polenta on each dish and spoon out some tasty sauce with mushrooms and sausages over top of each dish of polenta.

"When I grow up, I am going to open up a polenta restaurant and make everyone happy eating my special polenta," she said.

"Today is Saturday, Isabella; we will make the best-tasting polenta, Zia Maria's way," said her Zia Maria. She took the brand-new copper pot that she brought over from Italy and told Isabella to fill it halfway with water. "Now cover the pot and let us wait until the water boils," she commanded. Every once in a while, Isabella would uncover the lid to see if the water boiled.

Finally, the water sizzled and bubbled. Isabella called, "The water is boiling, Zia."

Zia Maria poured three cups of corn flour into the boiling water and then she stirred and stirred. As she was stirring, she chanted over and over:

> Gira, gira,
> lenta, lenta,
> buona, buona,
> mmm, polenta.

Isabella found this fascinating. She chanted along with her Zia Maria. Immediately the polenta started to thicken. She tapped the pot three times with the wooden spoon, and it was ready to eat.

Isabella put the beautiful tablecloth, from Italy, over the kitchen table. She filled up each dish with the polenta and then poured the tasty sauce with mushrooms and sausages over top each polenta dish.

"Mmm, mmm, this polenta is fit for a king, and a princess like you, Isabella," Zia Maria said. They all ate, until the pot was empty! Isabella was amazed at how much better it tasted than her mother's polenta.

"Next Saturday it will be your birthday, Isabella. You will be ten years old and you will make the polenta," said her Zia Maria. Her mother agreed. Isabella was so happy.

"Yes," she said and felt all grown up.

That day she invited her friends Leo and Alexa to her polenta birthday party. They were thrilled as they had never tasted polenta before.

Isabella got the large copper pot that her Zia Maria brought back from Italy and poured half the pot with water. Then she put the pot on the stove and waited until the water boiled. She placed the beautiful new tablecloth, from Italy, over the kitchen table, and put the dishes on the table. While they were waiting for the water to boil, her Zia told her that she needed to go to the store, and she would be right back. Her mother was going to be a little late coming home from work, but Isabella knew everything would be alright. She knew exactly what to do and would have everything under control.

Finally, the water was boiling. Isabella measured three cups of corn flour in the measuring cup and poured it into the boiling water. She took the wooden spoon and stirred and stirred the polenta. As she stirred, she chanted the same words her Zia chanted.

> *Gira, gira,*
> *lenta, lenta,*
> *buona, buona,*
> *mmm, polenta.*

"What does that mean," asked Alexa?
Isabella translated:

> Stir, stir,
> gently, gently,
> tasty, tasty,
> mmm, polenta.

Then all three of them chanted at the same time. They were having a good time. Suddenly the polenta thickened, and it was ready. Isabella stopped stirring but the polenta was getting thicker and was rising higher and higher over the pot. Isabella was astonished. It wouldn't stop flowing. It was pouring all over the stove. Then Isabella thought of getting it off the stove and put it on the table, but it kept flowing all over the new tablecloth.

"Oh no!" Isabella shouted. "This has never happened before." And it still kept flowing over. Now it was even flowing onto the floor. Alexa and Leo didn't know what to do.

"Maybe if we tell the polenta to stop, it won't flow anymore."

So, they all chanted "Stop, stop Polenta, stop," but that didn't help at all. By now it was pouring all over the floor.

Just then Zia Maria walked in and saw the mess. Immediately she took the wooden spoon, tapped the pot three times and the polenta stopped flowing. Her mother then walked through the door.

"Isabella, what have you done?!" she shouted.

Everything happened so fast that Isabella didn't know herself what she did wrong. She thought she did exactly what Zia Maria did.

"This has never happened before," she said. "I'm sorry." She put her head down and felt so ashamed.

Zia Maria took her aside and said in a whisper, "Isabella, you forgot to tap the copper pot with the wooden spoon three times after the polenta was ready. That tells the copper pot that the polenta is now good to eat, and it will stop bubbling over." Zia Maria realized she had forgotten to tell that to Isabella.

Everyone helped in cleaning up the mess, but there was still plenty of polenta in the pot to eat. Then Isabella had an idea. She took the tablecloth off the table and put her mother's pastry board on the table.

"Why don't we pour the polenta on the board and we can eat the polenta off the board," she said.

"Mmm, this is good," said Leo and Alexa.

As they were eating, they were having fun looking at the different shapes they were making with the polenta on the board.

Then Zia Maria brought in a delicious chocolate birthday cake and they all sang happy birthday to Isabella at her polenta birthday party.

And to this day they still eat polenta off the board, which has become a very traditional custom when eating Polenta in Italy.

The Stranger

What you are is God's gift to you;
what you do with yourself is your gift to God.

—DANISH PROVERB

THE JULY SUN WAS at its highest, filling the musty old church with unbearable heat. The village people were sitting at their regular places, rapidly fanning themselves with the paper newsletters, portraying an image of a silent movie. The humble priest, behind the wooden pulpit, was wrapping up the homily for the day.

The twelve-year-old altar server couldn't wait for the Mass to end. *When will Father Vincent install an air conditioner in this church? Everything is sticking to me, ugh!*

Exhausted from the heat, the jovial priest omitted his usual joke of the day. Beads of sweat rolled down his bony cheeks and settled within the creases of his dimples. He then announced the last song and chanted the closing words: "The Mass is ended. Go in peace."

Francesco impatiently took the long brass cross and carried it in procession with the priest down the aisle, leading to the door at the back of the church. The people gave their usual handshake and bid the priest farewell. Francesco hurried back to the altar, positioning the cross into its place. *This cross is getting heavier every week!* Then, in a silent prayer, he pleaded, *Please, God, don't forget I want a skateboard.*

Silence overtook the small Gothic church! All went home to continue their Christian lives, knowing they would be back next week, to worship and pray again. Francesco noticed everyone had left—that is, all except one.

A stranger, still kneeling in the pews, had caught his attention. *He must be sick*, thought Francesco. *No one stays in church after the eleven o'clock service.* He went over to the priest to inform him of the man left behind. The priest and Francesco hurried over to the stranger. "Is something wrong"?

"No."

The priest gave an inquisitive look. He seemed to have seen this man before.

The priest couldn't believe what he saw! It was a man with an unkempt beard and scruffy shoulder-length hair. His rough bronzed skin looked as though he had endured many hardships. His whole attire seemed as though it wasn't a good fit. The tattered navy blue suit looked worn out, and the faded jacket was slightly too big on his shoulders, looking a bit awkward. His frayed pants were quite short, with worn-out sandals covering his dusty feet. All the while the priest was conversing with him, the stranger never took his peaceful eyes off the cross at the altar.

Hey, this guy's nuts, wearing clothes like some sort of sophisticated beggar at church, and he doesn't even care what anyone says, Francesco thought. *Maybe he wants some money. I wonder who he is.*

Father Vincent asked, "What are you doing here?"

"I am worshipping the Lord! Doest thou not know me?" he answered.

Wow, he talks just like the people in the Bible, Francesco thought.

"What do you want?" the priest questioned.

"I have come to tell you that God loves us unconditionally," the stranger answered.

Francesco stood beside the priest, enjoying the conversation. Suddenly, this was more entertaining than swimming in his pool.

The stranger spoke calmly, without lifting his eyes from the cross. "Love the Lord with all thy might and love thy neighbor as thyself."

Francesco was mesmerized by the stranger's words. These words come straight from the Bible. *What if . . . ? Na . . . it couldn't be. Wow, he sure is weird*, he thought.

Suddenly the door of the sacristy banged open. The deacon cried out, "Father Vincent, the Catholic Women's League is waiting for you to say grace. You need to begin the luncheon."

"Yes" answered the priest quite relieved, "I'll be right with you." "Now I must ask you to leave. I need to attend the luncheon meeting. I don't have time for you at this moment. You understand, don't you?"

The stranger shook his head in agreement, stood up, and walked to the door. In the archway he turned, lifted his hand, and gave a humble wave. The priest and Francesco happily waved back. Francesco was disappointed that this weird moment had come to an end. He seemed to have some sort of unexplainable connection with him.

The stranger turned to Francesco and gave a final wave, and said, "Keep the faith, my son."

Suddenly the priest and Francesco became speechless. *No, impossible!* They ran after the stranger, pleading him to come back. But they were too late! The stranger had disappeared. Sweating, the priest and Francesco sat down on the steps outside the building.

Could it be? No! Impossible! They slowly got up, trudged back into the church. *Are those holes I saw in his hands?*

Francesco, curious of what he witnessed, arrived home. He slowly walked up to the porch. Then he stood paralyzed . . . he noticed the skateboard he asked for . . . laying on the front steps of his house!

Uncle Guido's Bag of Tricks

Our work brings people face to face with love.
—Mother Teresa

Francesco pushed his way through the huge glass door of the school and rushed to the bicycle stand, where Brian was waiting for him.

"Hey Francesco, do you want to go to the park and ride our bikes?" Brian asked.

"Not tonight; my Uncle Guido is coming over."

"The magician?"

"Yep, and he's bringing his bag of tricks to teach me some of his magic."

When Francesco opened the door at home, a cheerful man with a black derby hat, a black suit, and a little moustache waited for him.

"Uncle Guido, did you bring your bag of tricks?" Francesco asked.

"Oh yes, just for you."

That night, after a hearty spaghetti dinner, Uncle Guido grabbed his bag and pulled out some cards from a deck, placed them on the table face up like a fan, and said, "Francesco, pick out a card but don't show it to me; don't pull it out or point to it. Just remember what the card is and keep it in your mind." Then he gathered the cards and placed each card face up, one by one, in three piles from left to right. Then he said, "Francesco, point to the pile your card is in." He did this three times, and after the third time he went through the cards, when he got to my card he said, "This is your card."

Puzzled, Francesco asked, "How did you do that?"

"Let's do it again. Francesco, with this card trick you will only need twenty-one cards, so have your cards counted and ready before you start, then place the cards face up like a fan on the table. Ask the person to pick out a card, but do not pull it out or point to it; just keep the card you picked in your mind and remember the card you picked." Francesco picked the ace of hearts and kept it in his mind. Then Uncle Guido picked up the cards and placed each card face up, one by one from left to right, in a pile of three rows. "Now, Francesco, you have three piles of seven cards. Point to the pile where the card you picked is, then pick up each pile, but always pick up the pile you pointed to second, so that it will be in the middle of the three piles. Then do it again, three times, always remembering to gather the row that was pointed to second so it will be in the middle pile. Then go through the cards one by one, face up, and count out the cards in your mind until you get to the eleventh card." And there was Francesco's card, the ace of hearts.

"Francesco, this trick will never fail as long as you keep the row of cards pointed to in the middle pile when you gather up the cards. The eleventh card will always be the chosen card. This trick will always work—and remember not to shuffle the cards at all while you are doing this trick."

The next day Francesco couldn't wait to try it on his friend Brian and pulled it off perfectly.

"Here is another trick, Francesco, only this time it is with a coin." Uncle Guido put his empty hand to Francesco's ear, then showed him the palm of his hand. It had a coin on it. "Wow, how did you do that?" Uncle Guido explained, "Start with a coin hidden between your thumb and forefinger. Show that there is no coin in your hand, and then when you get to your friend's ear, drop the coin hidden from your forefinger onto the palm of your hand."

"It's so easy," Francesco laughed. "Gee, Uncle Guido, you're good."

"Francesco, magic tricks are by far one of the oldest forms of popular entertainment, and existed before television, movies, books, and theater. Magic tricks can enchant or fascinate your audience by creating illusions of impossible or supernatural performance using ordinary means. A good magician will mingle with his audience; keep them entertained by constantly talking and telling jokes to distract them from the trick. You may even come up with your own version, which can be even better than the original," said his uncle.

It was almost time for Uncle Guido to leave, but he left him with a few tricks with numbers.

"Pick a number between one and nine. Multiply it by three. Now add three, and now multiply the answer by three again. You should now have a two- or three-digit number. Add the digits together. Francesco, is your answer nine?"

"How did you know that, Uncle Guido"?

"No matter how many times you do this with any number between one and nine, your answer will always be nine. It's just the magic of numbers."

"One last number trick," he said. Look at the clock and choose any number on the clock. Now subtract the number opposite the number you chose. For example, if you chose nine, subtract three (which is opposite that number); your answer is six. You will notice that no matter what number you choose, when you subtract it with the number directly opposite it, the answer will always be six."

"Francesco, if you want to be a magician, age does not make a difference. Many years ago, magicians were taught as young as possible. By the time they grew up, they would have mastered tricks that require quick reflexes and certain techniques. You will be able to do magic tricks using simple materials such as a paper or pen, a deck of cards, or a hand-kerchief. Once you learn the secret behind the trick, you'll be amazed at its simplicity. Remember, practice makes perfect! Maybe the next time I come back, Francesco, you will be showing me some of your own magic tricks." They all laughed.

He gave Francesco a big hug, then left.

Francesco wasted no time preparing his magic show for his classmates at school!

www.ingramcontent.com/pod-product-compliance
Lightning Source LLC
Chambersburg PA
CBHW070944200626
46811CB00025B/1479